Querido dragón va al mercado

Dear Dragon Goes to the Market

por/by Margaret Hillert

ilustrado por/Illustrated by David Schimmell

NORWOOD HOUSE PRESS

Queridos padres y maestros:

La serie para lectores principiantes es una colección de lecturas cuidadosamente escritas, muchas de las cuales ustedes recordarán de su propia infancia. Cada libro comprende palabras de uso frecuente en español e inglés y, a través de la repetición, le ofrece al niño la oportunidad de practicarlas. Los detalles adicionales de las ilustraciones refuerzan la historia y le brindan la oportunidad de ayudar a su niño a desarrollar el lenguaje oral y la comprensión.

Primero, léale el cuento al niño; después deje que él lea las palabras con las que está familiarizado y pronto, podrá leer solito todo el cuento. En cada paso, elogie el esfuerzo del niño para que se sienta más confiado como lector independiente. Hable sobre las ilustraciones y anime al niño a relacionar el cuento con su propia vida.

Sobre todo, la parte más importante de la experiencia de la lectura es ¡divertirse y disfrutarla!

Shannon Cannon

Shannon Cannon
Consultora de lectoescritura

Dear Caregiver,

The *Beginning-to-Read* series is a carefully written collection of readers, many of which you may remember from your own childhood. This book, *Dear Dragon's Day with Father*, was written over 30 years after the first *Dear Dragon* books were published. The *New Dear Dragon* series features the same elements of the earlier books, such as text comprised of common sight words. These sight words provide your child with ample practice reading the words that appear most frequently in written text. The many additional details in the pictures enhance the story and offer the opportunity for you to help your child expand oral language skills and develop comprehension.

Begin by reading the story to your child, followed by letting him or her read familiar words and soon your child will be able to read the story independently. At each step of the way, be sure to praise your reader's efforts to build his or her confidence as an independent reader. Discuss the pictures and encourage your child to make connections between the story and his or her own life.

Above all, the most important part of the reading experience is to have fun and enjoy it!

Shannon Cannon,
Literacy Consultant

Norwood House Press • P.O. Box 316598 • Chicago, Illinois 60631
For more information about Norwood House Press please visit our website at
www.norwoodhousepress.com or call 866-565-2900.
Text copyright ©2012 by Margaret Hillert. Illustrations and cover design copyright ©2012 by Norwood House Press, Inc. All rights reserved. No part of this book may be reproduced or utilized in any form or by any means without written permission from the publisher.

LIBRARY OF CONGRESS CATALOGING-IN-PUBLICATION DATA

Hillert, Margaret.
  [Dear dragon goes to the market. Spanish & English]
  Querido dragón va al mercado = Dear dragon goes to the market / por/by Margaret Hillert ; Ilustrado por/illustrated by David Schimmell ; [translated by Eida del Risco].
    p. cm. -- (A beginning-to-read book)
  Includes word list.
  Summary: "A boy and his pet dragon visit the market and see all of the different foods and colors it has to offer. Carefully translated to include English and Spanish text "--Provided by publisher.
  ISBN-13: 978-1-59953-469-5 (library edition : alk. paper)
  ISBN-10: 1-59953-469-X (library edition : alk. paper)
  [1. Dragons--Fiction. 2. Grocery shopping--Fiction. 3. Spanish language materials--Bilingual.] I. Schimmell, David, ill. II. Del Risco, Eida. III. Title. IV. Title: Dear dragon goes to the market.
  PZ73.H5572114 2011
  [E]--dc23

                    2011016650

Manufactured in the United States of America in North Mankato, Minnesota.
178N—072011

Tengo que buscar algo
de comer.
¿Quieres ir conmigo?

I have to get something
for us to eat.
Do you want to go with me?

Sí, sí, mamá.
Quiero ir contigo.
¿A dónde vamos?

Yes, yes, Mother.
I want to go with you.
Where will we go?

4

Hay un buen sitio.
Ya verás.
Ven. Ven.

There is a good spot.
You will see.
Come on. Come on.

Oh, oh.
¡Mira todo esto!

Oh, oh—
Look at all this!

Puedes hacer esto.
Será una gran ayuda.

You can do this.
It will be a big help.

Sí, mamá.
Podemos ayudarte.
Nos gusta ayudar.
Será divertido.

Yes, Mother.
We can help you.
We like to help.
This will be fun.

Oh, esto luce muy bien.
¿Lo queremos?

Oh, this looks good.
Do we want this?

Habichuelas
Beans

Son HABICHUELAS verdes.

Sí, queremos algunas.

Las HABICHUELAS son buenas para nosotros.

These are green BEANS.

Yes, we want some.

BEANS are good for us.

Y mira aquí.
¡Qué ricas! ¡MANZANAS!
¿Podemos comprar
    algunas MANZANAS?

And look here.
Oh, boy! APPLES!
Can we get some APPLES?

Sí.
Vamos a comprar
        algunas MANZANAS.

Yes.
We will get some APPLES.

15

Los TOMATES son rojos.
Son ricos.
Vamos a comprar TOMATES también.

The TOMATOES are red.
They are so good to eat.
We will get
TOMATOES, too.

Tomates
Tomatoes

17

Ahora, ¿qué podemos comprar, mamá?

Now what can we get, Mother?

Miel
Honey

Jalea
Jelly

Mermelada
Jam

Calabacín
Squash

Cerezas
Cherries

Pepinos
Cucumbers

18

¿Te gustan las ZANAHORIAS?
Podemos comprar ZANAHORIAS

Do you like CARROTS?
We can get CARROTS.

Zanahorias
Carrots

¡Ay, sí! Me gustan las ZANAHORIAS.
ZANAHORIAS grandes y anaranjadas.

Oh, yes! I like CARROTS.
Big, orange CARROTS.

Allí hay algo amarillo.
MAÍZ amarillo.
¿Podemos comprar un poco de MAÍZ?

There is something yellow.
Yellow CORN.
Can we get some CORN?

Maíz
Corn

Supongo que sí.
Puedes ponerlo aquí.

I guess so.
It can go in here.

Quiero algo bonito también.
Busca algo bonito.

I want something pretty, too.
Look for something pretty.

Allí, mamá. Allí.
Mira que bonitas FLORES.
Puedes comprar FLORES.

Flores
Flowers

There, Mother. There.
See the pretty FLOWERS.
You can get FLOWERS.

25

Sí, vamos a comprar FLORES.
Ahora podemos irnos.

Yes, we will get FLOWERS.
Now we can go.

Flores
Flowers

Tú estás conmigo
y yo estoy contigo.
Qué día más bueno, querido dragón.

Here you are with me.
And here I am with you.
What a good day, dear dragon.

READING REINFORCEMENT

The following activities support the findings of the National Reading Panel that determined the most effective components for reading instruction are: Phonemic Awareness, Phonics, Vocabulary, Fluency, and Text Comprehension.

Phonemic Awareness: The /a/ sound

1. Say the word **apple** and ask your child to repeat the beginning sound. Say the word **can** and ask your child to repeat the middle sound. Say it slowly to help your child identify the middle /**a**/ sound.

2. Explain to your child that you are going to say some words and you would like her/him to give you a thumbs-up if s/he hears the short /**a**/ as in apple or can, or a thumbs-down if it is not the short /**a**/ sound.

ate (↓)	at (↑)	cap (↑)	cape (↓)
mat (↑)	mate (↓)	vane (↓)	van (↑)
sad (↑)	sand (↑)	grass (↑)	game (↓)

Phonics: Word Ladder

Word ladders are a fun way to build words by changing just one letter at a time. Write the word **am** on a piece of paper and give your child the following step-by-step instructions (the letters between the / / marks indicate that you are to give the sound as a clue rather than providing the actual letter):

- Add the /**b**/ sound to the beginning of the word. What do you have? (bam)
- Change the /**m**/ to a /**t**/. What do you have? (bat)
- Change the /**b**/ to a /**p**/. What do you have? (pat)
- Change the /**t**/ to an /**n**/. What do you have? (pan)
- Change the /**p**/ to a /**k**/. What do you have? (can)
- Change the /**k**/ to a /**f**/. What do you have? (fan)

Vocabulary: Story-related Words

1. Write the following words on sticky note paper and point to them as you read them to your child:

apples	beans	carrots	corn
flowers	orange	tomatoes	yellow

2. Mix the words up. Say each word in random order and ask your child to point to the correct word as you say it.

3. Mix the words up again and ask your child to read as many as he or she can.

4. Ask your child to place the notes on the correct page for each word, i.e. **apples** goes on the page apples are talked about.

Fluency: Choral Reading

1. Reread the story with your child at least two more times while your child tracks the print by running a finger under the words as they are read. Ask your child to read the words he or she knows with you.

2. Reread the story aloud together. Be careful to read at a rate that your child can keep up with.

3. Repeat choral reading and allow your child to be the lead reader and ask him or her to change from a whisper to a loud voice while you follow along and change your voice.

Text Comprehension: Discussion Time

1. Ask your child to retell the sequence of events in the story.

2. To check comprehension, ask your child the following questions:

- Why did the mother and boy put the wagon in the car?

- What did the boy and his mother buy that wasn't food?

- Where does your family buy food? How is it like the market in the story? How is it different?

Margaret Hillert ha escrito más de 80 libros para niños que están aprendiendo a leer. Sus libros han sido traducidos a muchos idiomas y han sido leídos por más de un millón de niños de todo el mundo. De niña, Margaret empezó escribiendo poesía y más adelante siguió escribiendo para niños y adultos. Durante 34 años, fue maestra de primer grado. Ya se retiró, y ahora vive en Michigan donde le gusta escribir, dar paseos matinales y cuidar a sus tres gatos.

Photograph by Glenna Washburn

Margaret Hillert has written over 80 books for children who are just learning to read. Her books have been translated into many different languages and over a million children throughout the world have read her books. She first started writing poetry as a child and has continued to write for children and adults throughout her life. A first grade teacher for 34 years, Margaret is now retired from teaching and lives in Michigan where she likes to write, take walks in the morning, and care for her three cats.

David Schimmell fue bombero durante 23 años, al cabo de los cuales guardó las botas y el casco y se dedicó a trabajar como ilustrador. David ha creado las ilustraciones para la nueva serie de Querido dragón, así como para muchos otros libros. David nació y se crió en Evansville, Indiana, donde aún vive con su esposa, dos hijos, un nieto y dos nietas.

David Schimmell served as a professional firefighter for 23 years before hanging up his boots and helmet to devote himself to work as an illustrator. David has happily created the illustrations for the New Dear Dragon books as well as many other books throughout his career. Born and raised in Evansville, Indiana, he lives there today with his wife, two sons, a grandson and two granddaughters.